MARIANNA COPPO

A VERY LATE STORY

FLYING EYE BOOKS

London | New York

Once upon a time, there was a blank page.

But it didn't stay that way for long.

???

Nobody knew how they got there,
or when. But most of all,
nobody knew why.

Um...

Calm down!
I think I know
where we are!

Huh?

Eh?

Oh?

Can we
play?

Ugh...
That's so boring!

Are we absolutely
sure that this story
is going to arrive?

I don't know.
Let's just wait
and see.

Sigh. In the old
days stories used
to arrive on time.

We'd better
just stay here.

And if it arrives
and doesn't find us?

What if we went
to look for it?

Well, at least
it isn't raining.

It sure is
making us wait,
isn't it?

FOR SALE

Yoo hoo!

GONE FISHING

Sorry I'm late!
I have something
here for you.

Here it is.
It's the story you've
been waiting for.

We've already
got one. Sit down and
we'll tell it to you!

Once upon a time, there was a blank page.